Transformers: Sam's New Car
Printed in the United States of America.
No part of this book may be used or reproduced in any manner whatsoever without written permission
except in the case of brief quotations embodied in critical articles and reviews.
For information address HarperCollins Children's Books, a division of HarperCollins Publishers, 1350 Avenue of the Americas, New York, NY 10019.
www.harpercollinschildrens.com
Library of Congress catalog card number: 2006935092
ISBN-13: 978-0-06-088823-7 — ISBN-10: 0-06-088823-7
❖
First Edition

TRANSFORMERS

SAM'S NEW CAR

ADAPTED BY E. K. STEIN

ILLUSTRATED BY VAL STAPLES

BASED ON THE SCREENPLAY BY ROBERTO ORCI & ALEX KURTZMAN

FROM A STORY BY ROBERTO ORCI & ALEX KURTZMAN

AND JOHN ROGERS

HarperEntertainment

An Imprint of HarperCollinsPublishers

Sam Witwicky wanted a car. Sam thought that if he had a car, kids might think he was cool. He worked hard in history class, and his teacher gave him an A minus. So Sam's dad agreed to help him pay for a car.

Sam and his dad went to a place that sold used cars. Sam wanted a new car, but they only had four thousand dollars to spend. "No sacrifice, no victory," his dad said.

"Cars pick their drivers," said the salesman. "It's a mystical bond between man and machine." Sam looked at all the cars, but he kept spotting one in particular—a beat-up yellow Camaro with black stripes.

The salesman noticed Sam looking at the yellow car. "It's your lucky day," he said. "I'll give it to you for four thousand dollars."

Sam sat in the driver's seat and turned the key. He was so excited—he had his very own car!

That night, Sam woke up from a sound sleep. He heard his car roar to life outside. Looking out his window, he saw his car drive off down the street. "Hey!" he shouted. "That's my car!"

Sam knew what he had to do. As the car sped through the neighborhood, he chased after it on his bike. He had earned that car—he was not going to let anyone steal it.

Sam pedaled as fast as he could, and followed the car to the edge of town and up to a closed gate. The car smashed right through the gate and then stopped suddenly. Sam hid behind some crates to watch.

Fog hung in the air, making it hard to see, but for a moment it cleared. Sam could not believe his eyes. The car had changed shape! It seemed like it had arms and legs. Then a bright light beamed from its chest into the night sky.

Trembling, Sam turned around and met two guard dogs face-to-face. The dogs growled and snapped their teeth. With a yell, Sam started to run away.

The dogs bit at Sam, and he tripped. Suddenly, with a roar, the Camaro skidded to a stop in front of Sam and honked at the dogs. The strange form Sam saw in the fog had vanished—it was a car once again. It honked and drove in circles until the dogs were scared away.

Sam backed away from the car, not knowing what to do. Then, just as suddenly, the car was gone.

The next day, Sam saw the Camaro parked back in front of his house. He thought his car must be possessed. He called his friend Miles and told him, "It's alive! My car . . . it stole itself, it walked, now it's back! I'm coming over!"

Sam hopped on his bike to go see Miles. He looked over his shoulder and saw the Camaro following him. Sam pedaled faster, trying to escape the yellow car.

Seeing a parking lot up ahead, Sam thought he could hide from the Camaro. He turned and raced into the lot. *SMASH!* He crashed into the door of a car—a police car.

"Help!" Sam yelled.

But there was no answer. Instead the car slammed forward, knocking Sam over. The headlights stretched out like snakes and circled Sam's face. Then the car transformed into a giant, sixteen-foot-tall, gray robot!

"This must be a bad dream," Sam said to himself. He was too scared to move.

"Have the Autobots seen the code?" The robot boomed.

"I have no idea what you're talking about!" cried Sam, who started to run.

The robot stomped after him and raised a gigantic fist. With a screech of tires, Sam's yellow Camaro appeared and crashed right into the gray robot, knocking him over. With the enemy down, the Camaro transformed into a yellow robot.

The gray robot rose and charged toward Sam. The yellow robot leaped in front to take the blow. He was knocked on his back from the force of the hit, but he quickly leaped up and grabbed a telephone pole, ripping it from the ground.

Using the pole as a baseball bat, the yellow robot swung at the gray robot and smashed him in the chest. Quickly transforming back into a Camaro, he popped open the door for Sam. As they drove off, Sam realized . . . his car just saved his life.

"Can you talk? What were you doing last night?" he asked the car. The car stereo turned on and flipped through stations.

A preacher on the radio called out, "A mighty voice will send a message, summoning forth visitors from heaven . . ."

"You were calling someone?" Sam asked. " 'Visitors from heaven?' Are you . . . an alien or something?"

Soon the car stopped on top of a hillside. Sam got out and stood beside him as he transformed back into a robot. Sam saw lights falling to the Earth. And, suddenly, his car was not the only robot in front of him.

Giant robots surrounded Sam. The largest one leaned down and said, "We are from the planet Cybertron. My name is Optimus Prime." Gesturing toward the yellow robot he added, "You've already met Bumblebee, guardian of Sam Witwicky."

"Bumblebee?" echoed Sam. In that moment, Sam knew he hadn't just found a new car—he'd found a new friend. An adventure awaited him.